PATRICK'S TREE HOUSE

by STEVEN KROLL
illustrated by ROBERTA WILSON

Macmillan Publishing Company
New York

Maxwell Macmillan Canada
Toronto

Maxwell Macmillan International
New York   Oxford   Singapore   Sydney

To the many moods of Maine.
— S. K.

Macmillan Publishing Company is part of the Maxwell Communication Group of Companies.
Macmillan Publishing Company, 866 Third Avenue, New York, NY 10022. Maxwell Macmillan
Canada, Inc., 1200 Eglinton Avenue East, Suite 200, Don Mills, Ontario M3C 3N1.

First edition
Printed in the United States of America

10   9   8   7   6   5   4   3   2   1

The text of this book is set in 13 point Berling.
The illustrations are rendered in pencil.

Library of Congress Cataloging-in-Publication Data
Kroll, Steven.
    Patrick's tree house / by Steven Kroll : illustrated by Roberta
Wilson. — 1st ed.
        p.   cm.
    Summary: When nine-year-old Patrick visits his grandparents in
Maine, he finds a surprise, his own tree house, but he soon has to
find a way to deal with two troubled boys who have taken it over.
    ISBN 0-02-751005-0
    [1. Grandparents — Fiction.   2. Behavior — Fiction.   3. Maine —
Fiction.]   I. Wilson, Roberta, ill.   II. Title.
PZ7.K9225Pat   1994
[Fic] — dc20   93-4571

Contents

1. Flying 5

2. Driving 9

3. The Tree House 15

4. Pancakes and Ponies 20

5. "Just Hold It Right There!" 24

6. To the Point 30

7. The Sign 35

8. Riding 38

9. Coming to Grief 44

10. Crossing the Line 49

11. A New Direction 52

12. Spooked 54

13. A Hard Bargain 58

14. Four Cans of Coke 60

1. Flying

"Bye, Mom! Bye, Dad!"

Patrick hugged his parents and dashed through the gate to the plane. He was nine years old, almost nine and a half. He'd never been on a plane by himself before, but he wasn't scared a bit.

Every August, Patrick and his parents went to visit his grandparents — his mom's parents, the Prescotts — in Maine. Every August, they took this very same flight. It lasted just one hour and landed right in Portland. There, Granddad met them and drove them another hour up the coast to the house.

Patrick found his seat by the window and stuck his backpack into the space in front of him. He settled in and fastened his seat belt. He glanced at the in-flight magazine, but was too excited to read.

Patrick's father, an eye doctor, was going to a convention of eye doctors the first week of the month. His mother, who taught English at New York University, was going along. Patrick would have more than a week with his grandparents before his parents even arrived!

A fat man in a plaid shirt and jeans sat down next to him. Patrick hoped he wouldn't start a conversation, but you

could never be sure. The fat man pulled out his newspaper and disappeared into it.

Patrick really loved his grandparents. Now that they were retired, he loved being able to spend more time with them. He loved their old house and his special room, called the Garret.

The flight attendant began explaining the safety regulations. Patrick listened and spied the nearest exit, two rows away. He took a deep breath and let it go as the plane roared down the runway and took off. He watched from the window as it rose into the sky above New York.

Patrick liked New York, but not in the summer. It got too hot and sticky, and day camp in July wasn't much fun. He loved escaping to Maine, loved the woods and the breeze off the ocean and his grandparents' two big ponies, Rufus and Gypsy. He wondered how the ponies were and whether his friend Sarah Washburn would be staying across the point this year. Sarah came from Boston. He'd promised to visit her there some day.

Two flight attendants came by with a cart full of things to drink.

"A Coke, please," Patrick said.

The flight attendant filled a plastic cup with ice and poured the Coke over it so that it fizzed. Then she handed the cup to Patrick, together with the rest of the can.

"Thank you," Patrick said.

He sipped his Coke, delighted he'd been given the whole can. On some flights you only got a cupful and had to ask for more.

By the time the flight attendants returned for the empty cups and cans, the fat man in the plaid shirt was snoring. A moment later, the captain announced over the intercom that they were about to prepare for landing.

The fat man's eyes shot open. He gripped the arms of his seat and began to perspire.

Somehow the fat man's fear made Patrick even calmer. He kept his hands in his lap, swallowed once when he felt the pressure in his ears, and sighed happily as the plane landed with a bump on the runway.

The fat man slumped over and dabbed at his forehead with a handkerchief. Patrick wondered if he should offer help, but there was nothing he could do. As the plane taxied in to the gate, he sat back and imagined how great it would be to see Granddad.

But he had to wait for the fat man, who seemed to take forever to pull down his garment bag from the overhead rack and walk unsteadily up the aisle. Patrick put his backpack on and followed, and then they were down the stairs to the asphalt and he was past the fat man and streaking for the door!

He saw Granddad the moment he got inside the airport. It wasn't hard to spot him. He was tall and thin, with a neatly trimmed gray beard, and he was heading straight for Patrick.

"Granddad!" said Patrick.

They hugged. Granddad lifted Patrick right off the ground and twirled him around. It was the best hug ever, Patrick thought.

2. Driving

When Patrick was down on the ground again, Granddad asked, "Well, how does it feel to be in Maine?"

"It feels great!" Patrick said.

Granddad smiled through his beard. "I was hoping you'd say that, my boy."

They walked over to the baggage claim. At first, nothing happened. Then one suitcase popped up out of the chute and rolled around on the circular conveyor belt, followed by another and another. But none of them belonged to Patrick. Was his suitcase lost? No, there it was. Granddad grabbed it from among the others, and they were off.

"How's Boris?" Patrick asked as they walked toward the parking garage. Boris was Granddad's ancient Oldsmobile Cutlass.

"Going good. I just changed the oil," said Granddad.

And there was Boris, big and green as ever. Granddad loaded the suitcase and Patrick's backpack into the trunk, the two of them strapped on their seat belts, and they were on their way, rolling up through Portland and north on Route 95.

Granddad held steady at fifty-five miles per hour, looking straight ahead and aware of everything on the road. He didn't believe in air conditioning, and the wind blasted through the open windows. Boris was just as Patrick remembered, so big and wide it was like riding along on pontoons.

"How's Grandma?" he asked.

"A little tired these days. She'll be better when she sees you."

"I can't wait to see her either."

The landscape opened out. The trees were almost all firs and birch. Every so often, Patrick got a glimpse of the ocean.

They spoke of the ponies, who had both turned thirty this past January first, and of "big, bad New York City," as Granddad called it. Patrick described his school, new this year, and how well he had done. It seemed okay to say something like that to Granddad.

Granddad smiled and gave the thumbs-up sign. "That's my boy!"

By then they were in Brunswick and switching over to Route 1. A silence followed, eaten up by miles of road. There was time to feel the leathery seats in the car, breathe the clean air blowing through the windows, and adjust to being in the country. Then Granddad turned off down a side road, and the trees closed in on them.

There was a pond on the left, then a village and a white church, but mostly there were trees, the familiar pine and birch, with the occasional oak or maple. Back in among them, usually a distance from the road, there were houses, but the quiet was so overwhelming, it was hard to believe people were actually there.

They passed the general store, made a couple more turns, and the road grew narrower. Finally, coming over a rise, Granddad made a sharp left and scooted down a long driveway that took them all the way to a clearing and the house.

It was such a friendly house, Patrick always thought: a neat, old Cape Cod with an L at the far end for the bathroom and another at the near end for the kitchen. The shingles were a weathered gray with white trim, the Garret was right above the kitchen, and the special stairway to it was just inside the kitchen door as you came in.

Granddad reached across Patrick and opened the car door on his side. "I've got a surprise for you," he whispered. "I'll show you after lunch."

"What is it?" Patrick asked, but Granddad only winked as Grandma slammed the kitchen door and came running down the porch steps to the car.

Quickly Patrick undid his seat belt, jumped out, and hugged her. She was warm and plump and cozy. "My goodness, Patrick, you certainly have grown."

Adults always seemed to be saying things like that, but when it was Grandma, Patrick didn't mind. Grandma was only just over five feet tall herself. He was almost as tall as she was.

"Four feet ten," Patrick said, "and that was a month ago."

"You'll be a man before we turn around," said Grandma. "We're so glad you're here. Come in and get settled."

Grandma led him inside and up the narrow stairs to the Garret. Granddad followed with the suitcase and the backpack. As Patrick reached the top step, he realized he was almost tall enough to duck.

The ceiling was low and slanted like the roof. There was a small room with a chair and a closet, then a slightly larger one with two beds, a desk, and a bureau. On one of the beds were Patrick's old teddy bear and a Mad Hatter doll.

"As soon as you're unpacked, come down for lunch," Grandma said.

Grandma and Granddad left. Patrick stood in the middle of the room. It smelled of woods and grass. Every time he came here, he wanted to stay forever.

Grandma had left the two small windows open and put a fan on the desk. Patrick turned on the fan and immediately felt cooler.

There wasn't much to unpack: some shirts, underwear, jeans and shorts, two sweaters, a bathing suit, a few pairs of socks. As he filled the upper drawers of the bureau, he wondered about Granddad's surprise.

Could it be a pet or something he had made in the shed? Maybe it had to do with the ponies.

The ponies! He missed them. He had to see them. He dumped the last pairs of socks into a drawer, put the suitcase in the smaller room, and clambered down the narrow stairs to the kitchen.

"Grandma, Granddad! Could I visit the ponies before lunch?"

Granddad was sitting at the kitchen table. He looked up.

"What do you think, Martha? Is there time for this rascal to disrupt the schedule?"

Grandma laughed. "Oh, I don't see why not. The peanut-butter-and-jelly sandwiches won't spoil in the meantime."

"Great!" said Patrick. He raced for the door.

"Just don't forget the apples from the crab apple tree," said Granddad behind him.

3. The Tree House

The barn was about a hundred yards from the house. It had big double doors and a paddock that snaked around behind it. On the way was a big crab apple tree.

Patrick ran to the tree. He ignored the apples already on the ground and picked two fresh ones. Then he ran to the barn.

Rufus and Gypsy were out in the paddock. They heard Patrick coming and rushed to the fence, their noses just high enough to poke over the top rail. When they saw he had apples, they flipped their ears forward and whinnied.

"Hi, Rufus! Hi, Gypsy!" Patrick shouted.

He fed them their apples from a flat palm, and they nuzzled and prodded him for more. Rufus was red and Gypsy black, but both their noses had turned gray. They were getting a bit tubbier, too.

"No more, not now." Patrick laughed, rubbing their foreheads and pushing their noses away. Then he patted both their necks. "Okay, that's it. I just wanted to see you guys."

He took off back to the house.

As he dashed through the door, Granddad said, "You were gone so long, my stomach has been grumbling."

Patrick screwed up his eyes and cupped his ear in his hand.

"Martha," said Granddad, "do you think our daughter is raising a wise guy?"

"I don't know, but let's eat," said Grandma.

The peanut butter was fresh and delicious, and the strawberry jam was homemade. The only odd thing in this country setting was the supermarket whole-wheat bread, Grandma's favorite.

Grandma knew that Patrick's parents served only bread from the bakery. He was ready for the next question.

"How's the bread?" Grandma asked.

"Delicious, Grandma."

"Bread's as good as fresh, isn't it?"

"Oh yes. Easier to handle, too."

Grandma smiled. "That's good. Thank you, Patrick."

What characters his grandparents were! Patrick finished his sandwich and washed it down with a glass of cold milk. He ate a peach for dessert — the sweetest, juiciest peach he had ever tasted. He was wiping his mouth with his napkin when Granddad said, "Are you ready?"

At first Patrick didn't know what he was talking about. Then he remembered. The surprise! Of course he was ready. He stood up.

Granddad stood up, too. They looked at Grandma, who was grinning. "Better get going. I'll do the dishes. The *two of you* can do them after supper."

"Okay," said Patrick, and Granddad smiled. He led his grandson outside and around the back of the house. They began climbing the path that went over the top of the hill.

Halfway up, Granddad stopped. "There," he said. "Have a look."

Patrick was confused. He peered into the woods and saw nothing. He swatted a mosquito. It was cooler here than in the clearing, but the mosquitoes would get worse later in the day.

"Look closer," said Granddad.

Patrick stepped off the path and peered again. And then he saw it: a tree house, big enough for two sleeping bags! Stuck up in a massive oak tree, it was braced by three large branches.

Patrick walked closer. Shingles covered the slanted roof. A six-foot rope ladder ran up from the ground to a trapdoor.

Patrick rushed back to his grandfather. "Granddad, thank you! You built this for me?"

"There wasn't anyone else to build it for."

"Can I try it now?"

"You're sure you don't want to wait till later?"

"No. I love it already."

Patrick dashed back to the tree house and up the rope ladder. He pushed the trapdoor open on its hinges and climbed inside. The space was high enough for him to stand in, except at the lower end of the slant. There was a small window at the lower end and a large window at the higher end, each with shutters to help keep out mosquitoes. Along one side was a table hinged to the wall. The whole thing smelled deliciously of fresh-cut pine.

It's perfect, Patrick thought, perfect.

He climbed back down the rope ladder and ran to his

grandfather. "Is it okay if I sleep out here tonight?"

Granddad laughed. "I thought the Garret was your favorite place. You haven't slept there once yet."

"This is even better."

That night, after helping Granddad do the dishes and talking to his parents on the phone, Patrick put on his pajamas. He borrowed Granddad's sleeping bag and the flashlight with the long handle. He packed up a plateful of the chocolate-chip cookies Grandma had baked for him. Then he went off to the tree house.

He slid everything through the trapdoor and climbed in after it. He unfolded the table and placed the cookies on top. He unrolled the sleeping bag, crawled inside, and gazed out the window at the night sky and dark trees.

Everything was peaceful. There were crickets chirping, but that was the only sound. The Garret had seemed private, but this small place, away from the main house, seemed totally his own.

After a while, Patrick closed the shutters and drifted off to sleep. Once in the night he was awakened by the hoot of an owl, and again by a squirrel skittering across the roof. Each time he just smiled and turned over.

4. Pancakes and Ponies

The next morning, Patrick ran down the hill and burst into the kitchen. "Grandma, Granddad, the tree house is great! I want to sleep there every night!"

"Well, maybe not every night, Patrick," said Grandma.

"I don't think you'll like it when it's cold," said Granddad.

"Well, maybe not when it's cold," said Patrick.

"Right now," said Grandma, "why don't we pay some attention to breakfast?"

She lifted the lid from a pile of steaming buckwheat pancakes.

"Yum," said Patrick.

"Dig in," said Granddad.

Everyone did. Patrick had a stack of three, smothered in thick Maine maple syrup, then followed it with a smaller stack of two. Grandma and Granddad weren't far behind.

"This Maine syrup," said Granddad between bites, "it sure is good."

"I always thought Vermont maple syrup was pretty good, too," Patrick said.

"You mean, until you tried Maine," said Granddad.

"Uh, yes, of course."

It was funny, Patrick thought, how everyone in Maine was convinced that something from somewhere else couldn't be as good as the same thing from Maine. Then again, everyone in Vermont probably felt the same way about Vermont.

When they were through and had cleared away the plates, Granddad said, "I have an idea."

"I know," said Patrick. "Let's call Sarah!"

Granddad chuckled. "Now how did you guess that? I didn't even move my lips."

"Oh, Granddad," said Patrick.

"I bet you didn't guess the rest, though. Assuming she's there, why don't we invite her for a pony ride in the wagon?"

A pony ride with Rufus and Gypsy was one of Patrick's favorite things. He hurried to the telephone table in the corner and looked up Sarah's number from last summer.

It rang three times. "Hello?"

"Sarah! It's you!"

"Patrick!"

They hadn't heard each other's voices for so long. It was great to hear them now. Sarah had had a good year at school to go with Patrick's good year. Sarah had already been in Maine for two weeks but, just like Patrick, would be staying through Labor Day. Her mom was staying with her the whole time. Her dad was coming up on weekends. Would she like to go for a pony ride in the wagon? Would she ever!

"Tell her we'll pick her up by eleven," said Granddad. "We'll have lunch here."

Patrick told her.

When he got off the phone, Granddad said, "Perhaps you'd better do something about those pajamas."

Patrick looked down sheepishly. He'd hardly realized he still had them on. "Right," he said, and ran upstairs to the Garret for jeans and sneakers.

When he got back and had cleaned his teeth, Granddad was ready to harness the ponies. "You boys have a good time," Grandma said as they tramped out the door.

Granddad put his arm around Patrick's shoulders. "It's a good thing I feed the ponies early, or they'd never be ready for this."

"Do you take them out a lot?"

"Not since last summer."

Patrick looked puzzled. "How will they be in the harness?"

"Don't know," said Granddad. "I guess we'll soon find out."

At the barn, Rufus and Gypsy were still in their stalls. Patrick helped Granddad place a wooden bar across the doorway and hitch the ponies to it. Then he helped attach the harness and the wagon and followed with the bridles.

"Kept everything in pretty good shape over the winter," Granddad said. "Thought we might be needing it about this time. Now I want you to hold Rufus's head. I'll hold Gypsy and slide the bar away. If they spring forward, just hold on tight."

Patrick imagined the ponies springing forward and tearing across the clearing. He imagined his grandfather and himself being dragged along after them.

But he did as he was told. Instead of springing forward, the ponies leaped back!

Patrick burst out laughing. So did Granddad.

"Well, I guess they had a better idea," Granddad said finally. "Poor old boys. They'd rather stay at home."

"Will they be okay?" Patrick asked.

Granddad patted them and settled them down. "Sure," he said, "once they get started."

They were better than okay. Patrick climbed onto the seat beside Granddad, Granddad snapped the reins, and Rufus and Gypsy trotted right out of the barn.

5. "Just Hold It Right There!"

Granddad drove the ponies across the clearing, then turned left onto an overgrown dirt road that led across the point. The road was barely wide enough for the wagon, but the ponies trotted right along, stepping over roots and stones as they went.

The woods were deep and dense, and there was no one in them but Patrick and Granddad. The wagon moved along at a steady pace, and the easy rise and fall of the ponies' haunches gave the journey a special rhythm. Then they were out of the woods in front of Sarah's house.

It was old, like Grandma and Granddad's, and covered with the same weathered gray shingles. It overlooked the bay.

And there were Sarah and her mom, running out to greet them. Patrick jumped down from the wagon. He said hello to Sarah's mom and Sarah.

"Hi, Patrick," Sarah said.

She smiled. She had long, dark hair and pale skin. Her hair was so dark, Patrick felt almost bleached beside her. He couldn't remember if he'd felt that way about his sandy coloring before.

Granddad went over the plans for the afternoon with

Sarah's mother. Then he said, "Okay, children, let's ride."

The ponies had been trotting a good ways, so Granddad let them walk to cool off. Sarah sat between Patrick and Granddad. Patrick felt proud of Rufus and Gypsy, proud of Granddad, and proud that Sarah was his friend.

Granddad flicked the reins over the ponies' backs, and they began to trot. Granddad had been right. They really were enjoying themselves now.

It was warm, but the breeze bathed their faces. The ponies' hooves made hollow sounds on the ground, and every so often, Granddad clicked his tongue and said, "Gee up."

Sarah held on to the seat and giggled. Then they were in the clearing and Granddad was saying he would take care of things in the barn.

Moments later, they were having lunch at the kitchen table. It was tuna fish on supermarket whole-wheat bread.

Patrick took a big bite. "Great bread, Grandma."

Grandma blushed. "Now Patrick, you stop."

Granddad snorted, but Sarah looked baffled. Patrick whispered he would explain later.

Afterward Patrick said, "I've got something I want to show you."

He took her straight to the tree house. He showed her how to climb the rope ladder and flip open the trapdoor. As he gestured for her to follow, he heard, "Just hold it right there!"

He looked up into the face of a kid about his own age. The kid was skinny and blond, with pale blue eyes and a tight mouth.

Patrick was horrified. Someone had sneaked into *his* tree house!

"Who are you?" he demanded. "What are you doing here?"

The boy glared down at him. "I'm Seth Dixon. This is my brother, Sammy."

Another boy emerged from the shadows behind him. Sammy looked exactly like Seth.

"We've taken over this tree house," Seth continued. "We don't like your face, we don't let you in."

Patrick had heard of the Dixon twins, who lived in the house across the road. He had even seen them from a distance. He didn't want to challenge them, but what could he do?

"This tree house is mine!" he said.

"Oh yeah?" Seth snarled. "Who says it's yours? I don't see any mailbox out front. I don't see any name on the door."

"Patrick, what's going on?" Sarah asked from the ground.

Still balancing on the rope ladder, Patrick looked over his shoulder. "Wait a minute, Sarah. We've got a problem."

He turned back to Seth and Sammy. "My granddad built this tree house. It's on his land. You better get out!"

"Ha, ha, ha," Seth said. "Fat chance. The way I look at it, finders keepers, losers weepers."

"But that's wrong —"

Before Patrick could finish, Seth flipped his fingers off the trapdoor and slammed it shut. Patrick winced from the noise and began to fall backward, then reached for the sides of the rope ladder and held on tight. For a moment he thought

27

about climbing back up and trying to force the trapdoor open. Then he climbed down to the ground.

He sat on a rock with his head in his hands. "We'll have to tell Granddad," he said to Sarah. "He'll come and get them out of here. If he can't do it, we'll call the police!"

Sarah sat beside Patrick. "Wouldn't all that make a terrible scene?"

Patrick glared at Sarah. He got up off the rock and started down the hill by himself. Shoulders hunched, hands in his pockets, he didn't look her way again.

Sarah waited a few moments. When she got to the bottom of the hill, Patrick was under a tree, staring at the ground.

"You're right, Sarah. What are we going to do?"

"I don't know, but it's still a pretty day. Why don't we walk out to the end of the point and talk about it?"

6. To the Point

"We'll have to ask Grandma and Granddad."

"Okay. Race you to the house."

"Go!"

They took off, laughing, across the grass. First Patrick was ahead, then Sarah. Coming around the corner of the house, they were neck and neck. They tumbled up the steps to the kitchen door and collapsed in front of it.

Grandma peered out at them. "Well," she said, "if I'd known you were racing, I'd have placed a bet."

"We both won," said Patrick.

"It was a tie," said Sarah.

"Then I guess I couldn't have lost. Do you want to come in or are you happier on these hard boards?"

Patrick thought of the boards in the tree house. The story of the clash with the Dixons was about to fly right out of his mouth. "Grandma," he said, "is it okay if Sarah and I go out to the end of the point?"

Grandma scrunched up her nose. "Your grandfather's back working in the shed, but I don't think he'd mind. And

I don't mind either, as long as you're careful on the rocks and are back by five."

"Great! Let's go, Sarah. Thanks, Grandma."

"Thanks, Mrs. Prescott."

They were off again, dashing across the lawn, past the barn. They waved at the ponies and started down the path through the woods. It was dark and cool and buggy. The tops of the pine trees stretched way up. The moss beneath their feet was soft and spongy. They helped each other over a fallen log.

The path emerged from the woods and ended. There was a drop and then the Prescott family beach, a small crescent looking out to the blue of the sea and an island beyond.

Patrick and Sarah skirted the drop and picked their way around the edge of the beach to the rocks that ran along the shore. The route was all ledges and crevices, with boulders sticking out here and there and the woods above. Sometimes there was a pool of water between crevices or a broken shell, cracked open by a hungry sea gull.

They leaped from ledge to ledge and crevice to crevice. It wasn't hard going, and the sunlight danced on the water. When they reached the end of the point and the ledges became more spread out and the boulders bigger, Patrick gestured to a hollow in the rock that looked like a chair.

"You can sit there if you want."

The chair was so big, Sarah looked tiny. Patrick sat beside her and gazed out to sea.

"I've been thinking. We *can't* tell Granddad. He'd be too upset. If he tried to do something, Seth and Sammy might

get back at him. If he called the police, they might still get back at him — and us, too!''

"But what if the Dixons try to keep the tree house?''

"We'll have to figure out something we can do ourselves. Of course, they could just leave.''

"After what Seth said?''

"Sure. Game's over, they've had enough fun.''

"I don't think so.''

"Neither do I. But they can't just move in and stay. What would they do for food?''

"One of them could guard the place, while the other one went for stuff.''

"But wouldn't they want to go home? They do have a home.''

"I guess so. I don't know. Why are they there at all?''

"How about a bomb? Small, fatal, two birds with one stone.''

"You'd lose the tree house, too.''

Patrick laughed. "You sounded so serious.''

Sarah put a hand over her mouth. "I guess I was, for a moment.''

"We could stand outside with a pan of fudge. The smell would lure them out, and we could beat them away with sticks.''

"They'd be back the next day.''

"They wouldn't like being tortured, though. Maybe they'd go somewhere else.''

"Don't count on it.''

"What can we count on?''

"Us."

"Yeah, us."

Patrick and Sarah slapped hands.

"We'll take care of them," Patrick said. "We'll show them they can't push us around." He sucked in his breath. "Can you come over tomorrow, Sarah? Maybe we can figure things out then."

"Sure, in the afternoon," Sarah said. "I'll ask my mom, but I know it's okay."

7. The Sign

After dinner, Patrick watched a Boston Red Sox game on TV with his grandparents. Grandma and Granddad were big fans. Patrick was really a New York Mets fan, but with the Mets in the National League and the Red Sox in the American League, it seemed okay to root for Boston when he was in Maine.

After the Red Sox pushed the winning run across the plate in the bottom of the ninth inning, Grandma and Granddad cheered. Granddad even stamped his feet. Then they all ate bowls of chocolate ice cream to celebrate.

When the bowls were washed and put away, Granddad said, "Well, time to turn in. Heading for the tree house, my boy?"

"Yes, sir," said Patrick.

Just like last night, he changed into his pajamas and picked up Granddad's sleeping bag. He was too full of ice cream to want any cookies, but he didn't forget the long-handled flashlight. It was very dark, and he would need it to light his way.

He kissed Grandma and Granddad good night.

"Watch out for raccoons," Granddad said.

Patrick started up the hill. The flashlight beam was the only spot of light in a dark landscape. Surely the tree house would be empty. It was after eleven o'clock.

When Patrick reached the rope ladder, he stopped — and heard noises! They were still in there, moving around and whispering.

Patrick couldn't believe it. Sarah's suspicions had been right. Maybe they *were* planning to stay in the tree house forever. But why weren't they expected home?

Patrick switched off the flashlight and strained to make out more of the conversation. It was all too faint and blurred. He switched the light back on and started down the hill.

He crept into the house. Maybe Grandma and Granddad would be in bed so that he could sneak right up to the Garret.

But Granddad was sitting at the kitchen table, drinking a last cup of the decaf he always drank late at night.

"What's the trouble, my boy?"

Patrick was still holding the sleeping bag and the flashlight. "I decided to sleep in the Garret."

Granddad knit his brow. "Why is that?"

"It's . . . too cold to sleep out there tonight."

It *was* colder than last night. Not by a lot, but colder.

Granddad leaned back in his chair. Of course he had said that Patrick wouldn't want to sleep in the tree house when it was cold. "I see," he said finally. "Go on up to bed then."

Patrick scampered up the stairs to the Garret. He was so embarrassed, he knew he was turning red. At least no one could see him now. Had Granddad noticed anything?

For an hour under the covers, he squirmed and worried.

36

Would Granddad talk to Grandma about his return? Would they ask him about it in the morning? What could he and Sarah do about the Dixons?

At breakfast nothing came up. Patrick ate some granola and smiled a lot. Grandma and Granddad seemed happy to smile back.

Finishing his cup of coffee — regular because it was morning coffee — Granddad looked out the window. "What a beautiful day. Another Maine special just for grandsons."

"Sounds good," said Patrick. "Would it be okay if I took a walk?"

"Of course, Patrick. Go right ahead."

Quickly, hoping he hadn't sounded too abrupt, Patrick went outside. He headed straight for the tree house, practically running as he followed the path up the hill.

When he got there, he walked all around, looking and listening. The Dixons had gone!

He started for the rope ladder. That was when he saw the sign taped across the trapdoor.

KEEP OUT! THIS MEANS *YOU!* the sign said.

Patrick was so mad, he wanted to scream. He knew he could get into the tree house, but the sign stopped him cold. Not only had the Dixons taken over his property, they were ordering him away from it!

8. Riding

Sarah came by right after lunch. Patrick heard the car door slam. "Excuse me," he said to Grandma and Granddad, and rushed out to meet her.

He cornered her on the lawn as her mother backed up the station wagon. "I've got to tell you something," he whispered, "before we go inside."

He told her about last night. He told her about the sign. As he spoke, her eyes widened.

"It looks hopeless," Patrick added.

Sarah shook her head. "No, no, no, it's not. But let's forget about the tree house for now. Could we ride the ponies?"

"I'll have to ask Granddad."

They walked back to the house. Grandma was washing up. Granddad was mending a china cup with a blue-and-white leaf pattern. He looked up as Patrick made the request.

"I suppose so," he said. "You are wearing jeans."

He glanced at their feet. "Sneakers. You know how I feel

about proper footgear for riding. Don't want anyone stuck in a stirrup.''

"I'll change," said Patrick, "but Sarah will be okay. She's a really good rider, and we'll stay in the paddock."

"All right," Granddad said, "but I'll be watching."

Patrick ran upstairs and put on his jodhpur boots. When they reached the barn, the ponies were munching hay in their stalls.

"Boys," said Granddad, "you're going to have some fun."

Rufus snorted and banged a hoof on the ground. Gypsy went on chewing. When Granddad hitched them to the rail, neither one looked very pleased.

"Would it be okay if I saddled Rufus?" Patrick asked.

Granddad narrowed his eyes. "You know Rufus is a rascal. You think you're up to it?"

Patrick nodded.

"Then let Sarah help you."

Patrick and Granddad took the English saddles and bridles from their hooks. Granddad got to work on Gypsy. Patrick smoothed the saddle pad onto Rufus's back, then placed the saddle neatly behind the withers and began tightening the girth. No matter how tightly he pulled, he couldn't get the strap beyond the second hole.

"Help me," he whispered to Sarah.

She pulled, too, but it was no use.

Patrick could feel Rufus's chubby belly, hard as a rock beneath the girth. "Granddad," he said, "Rufus is bloating up."

"You know what to do."

"I always think it will hurt him."

"It won't. I thought you said you were up to this."

Patrick clenched his teeth. "Okay, Rufus, get ready."

He kneed him in the belly — not too hard, but enough to make him feel it. Then he did it again.

Rufus looked around and nudged Patrick on the arm. Patrick could feel him letting his breath go, and he tightened the girth to the fourth hole, where it was supposed to be.

"Got it," Patrick said.

"Good going," said Granddad.

Flushed with success, Patrick picked up the bridle. Holding the straps in his right hand, he placed the bit in the four fingers of his left and pushed it up against Rufus's teeth. At the same time, he got his thumb in behind the teeth and pushed forward. Rufus resisted, but his mouth slipped open and the bit slid in. Quickly Patrick pulled the straps over the pony's ears and buckled the throatlatch.

Already Granddad was leading Gypsy toward the paddock. Patrick unhitched Rufus and followed. As they got outside, Granddad said, without looking back, "That's my boy."

Patrick smiled at Sarah. Sarah smiled at him. A moment later, they were in the saddle. As he flung his leg over Rufus's broad back, Patrick couldn't help but wonder about the tree house. What was going to become of it?

Granddad helped Sarah adjust her stirrups. Patrick adjusted his own. "All right," said Granddad, standing back, "go to it. Just remember, no one's been riding them for a while."

Poised in the saddle, Sarah kicked Gypsy gently with her heels. Gypsy moved out at a smart walk along the paddock fence.

Thinking he would fall in behind, Patrick gripped with his knees and kicked with his heels.

Rufus didn't budge.

Patrick tried again. He clicked his tongue. "Come on, Rufus."

Rufus put his head down and began nibbling grass.

"Rufus!" Patrick said. He pulled the pony's head up and kicked.

Rufus moved sideways, then stopped.

"Hold on a minute," said Granddad. He slapped Rufus on the rump.

Rufus dodged to the side, nearly unseating Patrick. Then he trotted forward and settled into a brisk walk. Sarah and Gypsy were just finishing their first tour of the paddock, and Patrick and Rufus began to follow them.

For the next half hour, Patrick and Sarah walked and trotted around the paddock. With her experience, she looked a lot better than he did. Gradually, though, Patrick began to feel more comfortable. Even his posting to the trot got better.

Eventually Sarah said, "Let's canter. Are you ready?"

"Sure," said Patrick, and kicked Rufus mightily as Gypsy took off across the grass.

But Rufus wouldn't canter, only trotted faster, then lurched into an awkward lope, and finally stretched out. He was cantering, catching up to Gypsy, and it was the most exhilarating moment of the day!

Together, they cantered twice around the paddock. Then they slowed down and stopped in the middle.

Granddad came forward. "Bravo, bravo, both of you; but I think that's enough for these old fellas. Come back anytime, though. You know they can use the work."

Patrick and Sarah dismounted. Side by side, they led the ponies to the barn. As they were putting the tack away, Sarah said, "Let's go to Beston's for fudge pops."

Beston's was a small store in a cove, with the best fudge pops anywhere.

Patrick smiled. "Let's."

9. Coming to Grief

Granddad said it was okay. They hurried along the driveway and turned left at the main road. Facing the traffic for greater safety, they walked one behind the other.

They'd gone only a little way when two running figures disappeared into the woods ahead of them. It was the Dixon twins, obviously heading for the tree house.

Sarah looked back at Patrick. He'd stopped by the side of the road.

"Look, it's okay," Sarah said. "We'll get them out."

Patrick shook his head.

"Think about the fudge pops."

Patrick imagined the icy chocolate flavor and the delicious pudding the fudge pop became close to the stick.

They began hurrying again. They passed the post office and some houses. After about a mile, the road dipped down a hill and turned into a loop, doubling back on itself past summer cottages. At the far end of the loop was Beston's Store.

From the top of the hill, you could see the ocean. Lobster boats bobbed here and there, along with the occasional sailboat. Patrick and Sarah paid no attention. They ran down the hill with one thing on their minds.

"Hi, Mrs. Beston," said Sarah as they crashed through the screen door. "Guess what *we* want!"

Mrs. Beston was a good Maine woman with a twinkle in her eye. "Hi, Sarah; now, let me see. Was it a wrench for the bathroom, an ironing-board cover, or, perhaps, a Tootsie Roll pop?"

Sarah giggled. "Silly. I always get the same thing. Patrick wants one, too."

Mrs. Beston reached into the ice-cream freezer behind the counter and pulled out two fudge pops, steaming because they were so cold. "I think these may be what you want. Nice to see you, Patrick. First time you've been in all summer."

"I just got here. Thanks, Mrs. Beston."

Usually Patrick liked spending more time in the store. Small as it was, it seemed full of everything imaginable, from toothpaste and shaving cream to potato chips, dog food, hip boots, magazines, a lobster tank, and the candy counter up front. He liked talking with Mrs. Beston, too. But right now he was interested in his fudge pop.

He and Sarah paid. They sat on the bench outside and pulled off the paper.

The thing about fudge pops was, they were so cold, your tongue would stick if you licked them. So you had to wait until they thawed a little. After that, you could do what you wanted.

Patrick had just taken his first bite when Fred Wilcox

appeared. Fred was a gaunt old fisherman who lived nearby. He said hello and went inside.

Patrick and Sarah went back to devouring their fudge pops. As they did, Mr. Wilcox and Mrs. Beston began a conversation.

There was stuff about the weather and how hard it was to find those old-fashioned Gillette blue razor blades anymore. Then Mr. Wilcox said, "You heard much about Ned Dixon and those twins of his?"

"Not since poor Kay died," said Mrs. Beston.

Patrick and Sarah looked at each other. They went on eating and listening.

"Ned's in a pretty bad way," Mr. Wilcox said. "It was all so sudden, he's beside himself with grief. Spends all his time working in that auto-body shop he built out back beside the garage. Leaves those cars all over everywhere. Can't find a minute to be with his boys."

"That's a shame," said Mrs. Beston. "A family needs to be together when there's a tragedy. Seems I've been hearing about those twins, too. Haven't they been in some trouble?"

"Yes, they have. Nothing important—missing school, sassing people, stuff like that. Kay did a real good job with them; they were always pretty nice kids. It's tough to be without your mother when you're nine, ten years old."

The conversation drifted away, but Patrick and Sarah were no longer listening. They had finished their fudge pops and were staring at each other.

"That's why," Patrick whispered.

"They needed somewhere to go," Sarah whispered back.

"But I still want my tree house!"

"Maybe they've left by now."

The two of them started home. Reaching the Prescott driveway in record time, they went straight up the path to the tree house. The trapdoor was shut, but the sign was gone.

"Seth, Sammy," Patrick called, "come out of there!"

Silence. Then a muffled voice shouted, "Go away!"

"If you don't leave my tree house, I'm getting your father!" Patrick yelled.

There was an uproar inside. Seth and Sammy came hurtling down the rope ladder and threw themselves on Patrick. Seth sat on his chest.

"Bring my father into this, and I'll bust your head!" he snarled.

Then the two of them disappeared up the ladder again.

10. Crossing the Line

Sarah rushed to Patrick's side. "Are you okay?"

Patrick sat up and held his head. It had all happened so fast, he hardly knew what hit him. "Yeah, I'm all right." He looked around. "Shirt's torn, though."

"I guess we'll have to tell your grandfather now."

At first, Granddad seemed angry. "All this was going on, and something had to happen before you let me know?" Then he sounded surprised. "That tree house is practically next-door, and we had no idea."

Finally, he had a suggestion. "It's a good thing you got off with nothing worse than a torn shirt, Patrick, but maybe we need to be kinder to these boys. Losing your mother is a terrible thing. Give them a little time, and see if they don't come around."

"What about my tree house?" Patrick asked.

"You didn't have it before. Another couple of days shouldn't make too much difference."

Patrick found another shirt, and it was arranged that Sarah could stay for dinner.

As she finished her noodles she said, "Maybe we should go to their house. We could talk to them, try to make them understand."

Patrick smiled triumphantly. "We could go after dinner. While it's still light."

"Well, I'm not sure," said Granddad. "Going over there so soon — "

"Please, Granddad," said Patrick. "It might be a good beginning."

After more discussion and special pleading, Granddad agreed that Patrick and Sarah could go if they were back in an hour. After an hour, he would call the Dixon house and go over himself.

That was fine with Patrick and Sarah. They hurried through the rest of dinner and raced outside.

The chill of a Maine evening had taken over the country-side. Late-afternoon light had dimmed to dusk. A race up to the tree house proved that the sign was back covering the trapdoor. Now, with the twins almost certainly at home, Patrick and Sarah had to do what they'd planned.

They crossed the main road and turned right, up the hill. At the top was the Dixons' driveway, and they started down it, passing those abandoned cars along the way.

Halfway down, Sarah stopped. "I'm scared, Patrick. What could they do to us?"

"Nothing. We're going to talk to them, remember?"

"What if they don't want to talk?"

"They will. I'm scared, too, but come on."

The red paint was peeling off the house. The front door was white but slightly askew. The lawn was so overgrown it looked as if no one had cut it since the spring.

Patrick and Sarah had gone past the Dixon property a

million times. Up close now, it had a special sadness.

No lights were on in the front windows. They crept around a corner and saw a light out back.

They stopped, but heard nothing. Patrick gestured to Sarah, and she followed him along the wall.

When they reached the back of the house, they stopped again. The light they'd seen came from the auto-body shop next to the garage. The doors were open. Mr. Dixon's legs were sticking out from under the car he was working on.

Patrick and Sarah could have told him the whole story. Instead, they hurried around the other side of the house.

Light was coming from two of the windows. Patrick and Sarah crouched beneath them, then straightened up enough to look inside without being seen.

It was the living room. Seth and Sammy were sitting on the shabby sofa, watching TV. The pale light from the screen flickered on their pinched faces.

"They look lonely," Sarah whispered.

"Should we knock on the door?" Patrick asked.

"I don't know. I don't think so. What do you think?"

"I want my tree house back."

"Let's go home. We'll think of something else."

Sarah pulled Patrick away. In moments they were being welcomed by Grandma and Granddad.

"So what happened?"

Patrick and Sarah explained. Everyone had to agree that at this point, giving the Dixon twins a little time might be the only solution.

11. A New Direction

The next day, Patrick had lunch at Sarah's. They ate hot dogs and hamburgers off the grill and didn't even talk about the Dixons.

So far this summer, they'd been to Beston's. Why not walk to the general store in the village for pizza? They decided to go the next day.

Once again, Sarah came by in the afternoon, and they set off. As they reached the top of the hill near the Dixon driveway, Seth and Sammy were coming toward them on the same side of the road.

"What'll we do now?" Sarah asked.

"The best we can," Patrick replied.

Seth and Sammy walked right up to them. Seth folded his arms. "Why are you blocking our way?"

"We're not," said Patrick. "We're taking a walk."

"You want to walk, you walk on your side."

Patrick frowned. "It's a free country. We can walk where we want on a public road."

"Oh, yeah? Is that so?"

Seth pushed Patrick. Then he pushed him again.

"Look—Seth—cut it out," Patrick said. "Can't we just talk to you?"

Seth grabbed Patrick by the collar. "We don't want to talk!" Seth's eyes blazed. His breath was in Patrick's face.

"Seth!" Patrick shouted. He pulled those hands away. Seth was so surprised, he fell. Patrick jumped on him.

Sammy lunged forward, but Sarah butted him in the stomach. He sat down with an "Oof."

"Now *I'm* going to talk," Patrick said.

Seth squirmed beneath him. "You still can't have the tree house back."

Patrick pinned Seth's arms. He leaned over him in the grass and got an idea. "We don't want it back. We want to be friends."

Seth laughed.

Patrick looked at Sarah. "Friends are better than enemies."

Seth looked puzzled, then maybe a little pleased. "I guess you're right about that." Sammy was getting to his feet. "What do you think, Sammy?"

Sammy shrugged.

"You guys ever been riding?" Patrick asked.

"Never," Sammy said.

"Come ride our ponies, Rufus and Gypsy, tomorrow afternoon."

Seth brightened some more. "That sounds like fun."

"Good. Show up at three. Wear jeans and hard shoes. Granddad won't let you ride in sneakers."

"Okay," Seth said. "There's just one thing."

"What's that?"

"You'll have to let me up first."

12. Spooked

Patrick and Sarah scrambled down the hill to tell Grandma and Granddad.

"Do you think they'll come?" Patrick asked on the run.

"Beats me," said Sarah, "but it's worth a shot."

Granddad shook his head. "I have to hand it to you kids. I never thought you'd do that."

But they had, they had! The pizza at the general store tasted extra good that afternoon.

The next morning, Sarah had to help her mom do the grocery shopping in town. She didn't arrive at the barn until just after three. Believe it or not, the twins were already there, standing in a corner as Granddad saddled Gypsy and Patrick struggled to saddle Rufus. They were wearing freshly washed jeans and their good black shoes.

When both the ponies were ready, Patrick and Granddad led them out to the paddock and put the reins over their heads.

"Okay, Sammy," Granddad said, "you come over here and get on Gypsy. Patrick, you help Seth."

Looking almost sheepish, the Dixons obeyed. Patrick explained to Seth how you mount from the left side, facing the rear of the horse, with the stirrup turned toward you. That way, if the horse starts to move as you get on, the momentum carries you onto its back.

Seth folded his arms and nodded.

Patrick demonstrated. He took the reins in his left hand, put his left foot in the stirrup, and swung on.

"Doesn't look hard," Seth said.

He tried it. No problem. Patrick adjusted his stirrups and showed him how to hold the reins. He explained about gripping with your thighs and knees and how you didn't pull on the reins so much as squeeze them.

Sammy was ready about the same time. "Sarah," said Granddad, "why don't you lead Gypsy. Patrick can stay with Seth."

Sarah went first, walking right along, holding Gypsy by the bridle. Patrick followed, and they went twice around the paddock.

"Both of you look fine," Granddad said. "Sarah, Patrick, let them walk by themselves."

As Patrick let go of Rufus's bridle, he felt a twinge of fear. Would Rufus stop walking? Would he do something weird? He remembered what had happened the other day.

But Rufus went on following Gypsy. Slowly, carefully, rocking a little in their saddles, Seth and Sammy rode three times around the paddock.

"Can't we go any faster?" Seth shouted.

Patrick looked at Granddad, who nodded. Patrick went over to Seth and Sammy and got them to stop.

"If you want to trot, you'll have to learn to post. Every

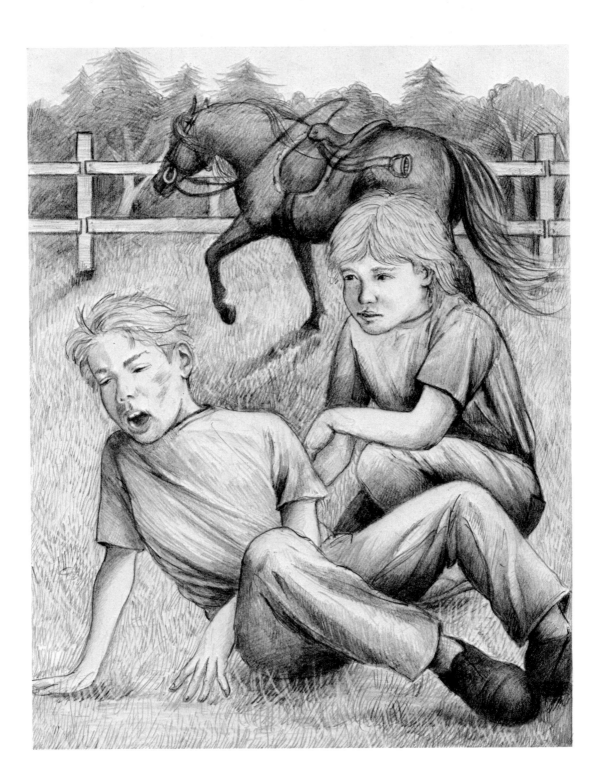

time the pony's inside front foot moves forward, move up and a little forward in the saddle. You'll bounce around at the start, but once you get the hang of it, you'll never forget how.''

Patrick had them practice at a walk, gripping and rising, gripping and rising. "Okay," he said finally, "give it a try."

Sammy kicked Gypsy into a walk, then kicked him harder and began an easy trot. Immediately he began bouncing around, but he kept on going, kept on struggling.

Rufus didn't move. Suddenly Seth shouted, "Hey!" He kicked Rufus with all his might and struck him with his fist.

Spooked, Rufus took off across the paddock. Off-balance from his punch, Seth was hurled backward. His feet flew out of the stirrups, and he tumbled to the ground.

Patrick and Granddad got there first. Sarah was a moment behind. Seth was lying on his side. Patrick touched his shoulder. "Are you all right?"

Seth stood up. A spot of dirt soiled his cheek. His jeans were ripped. His black shoes were scuffed and dirty.

"You did this on purpose," he snarled. "You only wanted to embarrass me. Sammy, we're leaving!"

There was a stunned silence. Then Sammy dismounted, and the twins were gone.

13. A Hard Bargain

Back at the house, Patrick couldn't stop talking about what had happened. He should have said more about what Rufus was like, but how could Seth behave so badly? They'd never get the tree house back now!

Granddad took him by the shoulders. "Hey, hey, whoa. First of all, you didn't do anything wrong. Second, you can always try again."

"It's all ruined, Granddad!"

"No, it's not. In fact, why don't you go over there right now and tell Seth that the whole thing was just a misunderstanding? Sarah will stay here and wait for you."

"You can invite those boys to a picnic lunch on our beach tomorrow," Grandma added.

Patrick stood up. "All right. I don't know if I'll get anywhere, but I'll go."

He climbed the hill to the Dixon driveway. He walked past the abandoned cars. He knocked on the front door.

No one answered. He tried again and heard feet shuffling. He hoped it wouldn't be Mr. Dixon. How would he explain to him?

The door opened. It was Seth, standing in his socks. When he saw who it was, he tried to close the door again. But Patrick wouldn't let him. He slammed his shoulder against Seth's weight, and the door burst open.

Seth ran down the hall. "You leave me alone! Sammy, help!"

Patrick could hear the TV blaring in the living room. He tackled Seth before he could get there. They rolled around for a moment, but Patrick climbed on top.

He pinned Seth's arms. "Why do I always have to talk to you this way? Can't we talk like normal people?"

"You made me look stupid! I hate you!"

Patrick explained about Rufus. "But you didn't have to be such a creep!" he added.

Seth calmed down. "All right. What do you want now?"

"I want you and Sammy to come to a picnic lunch on our beach tomorrow at twelve-thirty."

Seth's eyes narrowed. "Yeah, we'll come. I'd never dodge a free meal. Now — off!"

Patrick stood up.

Seth brushed at his clothes and shrugged.

"I'll see you tomorrow," Patrick said.

14. Four Cans of Coke

The day dawned cool and damp and overcast, but like many Maine days, it didn't stay that way for long. By noon it was warm, and if it wasn't exactly sunny, at least the sun was trying to break through the clouds.

Patrick felt relieved. A picnic in the house would have been terrible.

Grandma was busy humming and packing the picnic basket until just before twelve-thirty. There were fresh-baked brownies, apples, and chicken-salad sandwiches on supermarket whole-wheat bread. There were Cokes and — if anyone should want such a thing — milk.

At promptly twelve-thirty, the Dixon twins appeared on the lawn. Everyone seemed surprised by this except them. They said hello, called Granddad and Grandma Mr. and Mrs. Prescott, and shook hands. A moment later, Sarah's mom drove up and dropped Sarah off.

"Well," said Grandma, "let's hit the beach. I'm starved."

Before anyone could blink, Seth offered to carry the picnic basket. Grandma smiled. "Why, certainly, Seth. Thank you so much."

Patrick was flabbergasted. Then Sammy picked up the cooler with the drinks, and everything seemed even more unlikely.

Patrick, Sarah, and Granddad carried the towels — in case anyone was bold enough to swim in the cold water — and a tarpaulin to sit on. On the way down the path through the woods, Seth and Patrick walked together.

Immediately, though a little awkwardly, Seth started asking about life in New York. Did Patrick really live in an apartment? Did he go to parks and museums?

Patrick answered all the questions. Then he asked Seth about what Maine was like in the winter.

"No," Seth said, "it doesn't snow all the time, and, yes, people do go out, even when it's real cold. Traveling around isn't so bad because the snowplows keep the roads pretty clean."

The sky still hadn't cleared when they reached the beach, but no one seemed to care. The light on the water sparkled, and Grandma unpacked the food.

Everything tasted so good, it was gone in an instant. Afterward, the four kids sat together on the tarpaulin, still drinking their Cokes. They'd been talking about school, but when Sarah said something about her school play, Patrick said, "Yeah, I wish my dad had come to mine. He was too busy. Too many patients."

"We don't see much of our dad, either," Sammy said.

Patrick knew he'd been misunderstood, but he didn't say so. "It's hard," he said instead.

"It's hard for me, too," Sarah said. "The whole summer, I only see my dad on weekends."

A conversation began about dads. Sarah's dad was funny. Patrick's was a little stiff. Seth and Sammy were vague, then admitted theirs wasn't very nice to them sometimes.

"Hey," Patrick said, "why don't we go to the tree house? I mean, just to finish our Cokes."

Seth and Sammy looked panicky. "I don't think that's a good idea," Seth said.

"Oh, come on," Patrick said. "It's too big to run off with."

Seth looked at Sammy. "Maybe for a couple of minutes."

Granddad nodded. The four kids hiked back through the woods and up the hill. When they reached the tree house, Seth took the sign off the trapdoor.

"You first," he said to Patrick.

Patrick smiled. "Thanks." He let Sarah go up the rope ladder ahead of him.

Inside, the place was empty and untouched. The intruders hadn't seemed to know what to do to make it theirs.

When Seth and Sammy had climbed in, the four sat in a circle.

"You know," Seth said, "Sammy and I talked this morning. We decided to try and be nice to you guys. It wasn't as tough as we thought. You aren't so bad."

"Neither are you," said Sarah.

Sammy grinned, and Patrick said, "What do you think? Can we share the tree house?"

Seth shrugged. "Sounds good to me. We know the place is really yours."

Patrick held up his can of Coke. "To all of us together."

"Together," Seth said.

Then they all clinked cans and drank.